Dealing with....

DIVORCE

by Jane Lacey

Illustrated by Venitia Dean

PowerKiDS
press.

Published in 2019 by **The Rosen Publishing Group, Inc.**
29 East 21st Street, New York, NY 10010

Cataloging-in-Publication Data

Names: Lacey, Jane. | Dean, Venitia, illustrator.
Title: Divorce / Jane Lacey; illustrated by Venitia Dean.
Description: New York : PowerKids Press, 2019. | Series: Dealing with... | Includes glossary and index.
Identifiers: LCCN ISBN 9781538339039 (pbk.) | ISBN 9781538339022 (library bound) | ISBN 9781538339046 (6 pack)
Subjects: LCSH: Divorce--Juvenile literature. | Children of divorced parents--Juvenile literature. | Divorced parents--Juvenile literature.
Classification: LCC HQ814.L33 2019 | DDC 306.89--dc23

Editor: Sarah Peutrill
Series Design: Collaborate

Manufactured in the United States of America

CPSIA Compliance Information: Batch #CS18PK: For Further Information contact Rosen Publishing, New York, New York at 1-800-237-9932.

Contents

MY HOME ISN'T A HAPPY PLACE TO BE ANYMORE

Holly's mom and dad argue a lot. They never seem to smile or laugh or have fun. Holly's home isn't as happy as it used to be.

Luli is Holly's friend

Holly's my best friend but she never invites me over to her house. She always wants to come home with me. She says she wishes my mom and dad were her mom and dad.

Luli

Holly's story

Mom and Dad keep shouting at each other. Sometimes they just don't talk.

If I want to talk to them or give them a hug, they say, "Go away, Holly! Not now, Holly! Later, Holly."

They never have time for me.

My friend Luli's mom and dad are always smiling.

When I come over to play, they say, "Hello, Holly. It's lovely to see you."

They take us swimming and we go to the park. Luli's mom cooks delicious food.
We laugh and have fun.

She can:

★ try to talk to her mom and dad when they aren't arguing or busy

★ tell them how she feels - that she wishes they had more time to spend with her and she wants them all to have fun together

What Holly did

I talked to Mom and Dad. They said sorry. They said they made each other unhappy, but they did not want to make me unhappy, too. Luli came over and Mom took us to the park. We had my favorite, spaghetti and meatballs, for dinner.

We had fun, but I think Mom and Dad are going to get a divorce.

It helps to talk to your mom or dad.

Before my husband and I got divorced, we were very unhappy. We were too busy arguing to notice that our son Chris was unhappy, too.

So when Chris told us that he wanted to leave home and live with his grandparents, we were shocked!

But we were glad Chris told us how he was feeling. It meant we could help him to feel better. We tried not to argue in front of Chris. We made sure we still had happy times with him.

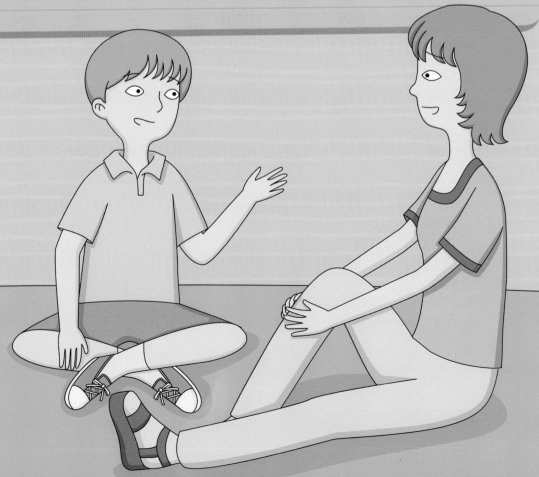

WHAT IS DIVORCE OR SEPARATION?

Parents split up, or separate, when they decide not to live together anymore. If they are married, they can get a divorce. They sign papers that make them single, or not married, again.

After parents split up, children usually live with one of their parents and visit the one they are not living with. A judge may help to make sure this is fair.

Parents split up from each other, not their children. They will always be their children's parent. It is never the children's fault.

MY PARENTS ARE GETTING A DIVORCE

Billy knows his parents are getting a divorce, but he doesn't understand what it means. It makes him feel worried and afraid.

Billy's story

Mom and Dad are getting a divorce but they didn't tell me much about it. My friend Joe's parents got divorced, but I haven't asked him about it. I'm afraid divorce means something bad will happen.

What can Billy do?

He can:

* ask his parents to tell him what divorce means
* say he is worried about what will happen
* talk to his friend Joe

What Billy did

I asked Mom and Dad what divorce meant and they explained. They said they would make sure I agreed about what happened to me.

I talked to my friend Joe. He told me that things had worked out all right for him. I feel better now about what's going to happen.

Joe is Billy's friend

When my mom and dad got divorced, Dad moved out and I stayed with Mom.

I see Dad nearly every Sunday and we go out together. We talk on the phone or email almost every day.

He's buying a house so I'll be able to stay with him soon. We're going away together on vacation in the summer.

Mom works and sometimes Grandma picks me up from school. Things have changed but it's OK. It's not as bad as I thought it was going to be. Dad and I still have fun.

I FEEL ANGRY WITH MY MOM AND DAD

Gracie's parents are splitting up. She feels angry with them for letting it happen. She thinks they should try harder to get along with each other.

Gracie

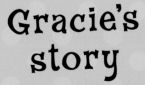

Gracie's story

I feel really angry with Mom and Dad. They are going to split up and they are ruining everything!

When my sister and I argue, they tell us to say sorry and be friends! Why can't they do the same?

What can Gracie do?

She can:

★ tell her parents how she feels about the separation - that she is angry with them and thinks they should make up
★ listen to what her parents say

What Gracie did

I told Mom and Dad they were ruining everything. I said, "Why do you have to split up?"

They said they had tried hard to work things out.

They were sad they were splitting up, too. I don't feel so angry with Mom and Dad anymore.

I am still sad they are splitting up, but at least it will make them happier.

Alfie was also angry when his mom and dad split up.

Last year, my dad left my mom, me and my little sister and went to live with his girlfriend. I was really angry.

Now my little sister and I are supposed to visit Dad every other weekend. I wouldn't go at first. I was so mad at Dad. He shouldn't have left us!

But Mom said she wanted me and Dad to be friends. Now Dad and I have tennis lessons together. We went to the beach last weekend. We have a nice time, but I still haven't been to his new home. Maybe I will go there soon.

IS MY PARENTS' DIVORCE MY FAULT?

Rosa worries that it's her fault her parents are getting a divorce. She thinks she can keep it from happening by always being kind and good.

Mo   Rosa

Mo is Rosa's friend

Rosa and I used to have lots of fun. Sometimes we were really silly and got the giggles.

But she's changed. She never wants to be silly anymore. She even worries about little things like getting her clothes dirty or making a spelling mistake. I don't know what's the matter with her!

15

I haven't told anyone, but Mom and Dad are splitting up. Dad's going to leave home.

Sometimes I can get in trouble. I'm worried that it's my fault they are splitting up. I want to make things better so Mom and Dad will be happy together again. I make them cards and presents, I clean up my room, I work hard at school. I don't argue with my younger brother and sister.

I think that if I'm very good, maybe they won't get divorced and Dad will stay with us.

She can:

★ talk to someone she trusts, such as her friend Mo, her grandparents, or her teacher
★ remember that her parents' divorce is not her fault
★ tell her parents how she feels

What Rosa did

I talked to my friend Mo. She said when her mom and dad got a divorce, they told her it wasn't her fault. She said it's not my fault either.

There's nothing I can do to make my mom and dad stay together. I wish there was, but at least I don't have to be perfectly behaved all the time, after all!

WHAT'S GOING TO HAPPEN TO ME?

Ed is worried about what is going to happen to him when his parents split up. He thinks everything will change. He doesn't think any of the changes will be good ones.

Sangita is Ed's friend

Ed thinks we won't be friends after his mom and dad split up.

He's worried he'll have to move to a new house and go to a different school.

But I think we can always be friends, whatever happens.

Ed's story

I know my mom and dad are splitting up but I don't know what's going to happen to me.

Where will I live and who will I live with – Mom or Dad?

If we have to move, will my new home be as nice as this one?

Will we have enough money?

Will I have to change schools?

Can I still play on the soccer team?

Will I lose all my friends?

Will I still see Gran and Granddad?

I'm worried about everything!

What can Ed do?

He can:

★ talk to his mom and dad about his worries - things might not be as bad as he thinks

★ talk to his friends and make plans to keep in touch - they can talk on the phone, email, and visit each other

What Ed did

I asked Mom and Dad what was going to happen. They said we were going to sell our house but they didn't know where my new home would be.

They said if I did change schools I would make new friends. They've promised to help me keep in touch with my old friends and play soccer. I'll still see Gran and Granddad.

Sometimes, parents who are separating or getting a divorce can't agree on what to do about money and their children. When that happens, a mediator can help.

A mediator's story

An important part of my job is to listen. I listen to both parents and I listen to the children. I help them all to listen to each other.

They all say what they want to happen and what they think is fair.

I help them to make the best plan they can, even if it isn't perfect.

I'M ASHAMED ABOUT MY PARENTS' DIVORCE

Louis feels ashamed. He does not want his friends to find out that his parents are divorced.

Louis's story

Louis

I don't want my friends to know what has happened at home. I pretend Dad is still living with us. I don't ask my friends over to my house in case they find out he's gone.

I flew my kite with my friend yesterday. I pretended I was happy and I didn't tell her what is happening. I feel ashamed my family doesn't live together anymore.

Louis's teacher's story

Louis should not be ashamed at all. Many children have parents who have split up. Louis certainly isn't the only one. It has happened to several other children in my class, too. No one thinks any worse of them because of it.

He can talk to me about it. He can talk to one of the other children whose parents are divorced.

Keeping a secret can make you feel unhappy. It can really help to talk about what is happening to you.

HOW CAN I LOVE BOTH MY MOM AND DAD?

Now that Darcy lives with her mom and just visits her dad, she worries that she won't be able to love them both the same.

Lily is Darcy's friend

Darcy lives next door. I play with her after school and on weekends.

She keeps worrying about her dad. She thinks she should keep him company and not be having fun here with me.

Lily

Darcy's story

After my parents split up, Dad went to live in an apartment. My sister and I and our pets live with Mom.

I think Dad is lonely and misses us all. I feel bad when I'm having fun when he is on his own. I think I should be with him to cheer him up and keep him company.

But if I lived with Dad, then Mom and my sister would miss me. I'd miss them, too.

I don't know what to do. I want everyone to be happy!

Darcy

She can:

★ talk to her dad on the phone and tell him her news
★ send him emails, letters, pictures, and photos that will make him smile
★ ask her dad to do the same for her

What Darcy did

Sometimes I call Dad and sometimes he calls me to talk. He says my pictures and letters cheer him up. He tells me nice things he is doing so I don't worry about him.

When I visit, I sometimes take our dog Buster, and we all go for a walk.

WILL WE BE HAPPY AGAIN?

When parents split up, it can be upsetting for everyone in the family. But things usually work out for everyone in the end.

Fred's story

When Mom and Dad split up, the whole family was upset. I didn't think I'd ever be happy again! I thought I wouldn't see Mom after she moved out. I thought Dad wouldn't be any good at looking after us.

But I see Mom lots and we send emails every day, too. Dad isn't such a bad cook after all! I know Mom will always be my mom and Dad will always be my dad and they'll always love me, whatever happens.

IT HAPPENED TO US

Henry and Ally's parents' divorce was very upsetting, but now everything is much better.

Henry and Ally's story

Henry:

One day, my sister Ally and I had a big fight, I can't remember why.

Ally:

Dad really shouted at us. Then Mom shouted at us. Then Dad and Mom got in a fight.

Henry:

I said to Ally, "Do you think Mom and Dad are going to split up?"

Ally:

I said, "If they do, it's our fault because we're bad and we keep fighting!"

Henry:

But Mom and Dad said, "It's not your fault we're getting a divorce."

Ally: We stopped fighting and being bad, but it didn't make any difference.

Henry: Mom and Dad got a divorce anyway. We were really worried and unhappy. We didn't want things to change.

Ally: We moved to a smaller house but we stayed at the same school. Dad moved out but he didn't go far away.

Henry: We talk to Dad on the phone or email him nearly every day. We have fun when we stay with him.

Ally: Mom and Dad met new people and have new partners now and they've got children, too. Now we're part of a really big family!

Henry: Things have worked out OK. It's much better than we thought it would be.

GLOSSARY

Ashamed
When you feel ashamed you are embarrassed. You don't want anyone to know something about you so you keep it a secret.

Divorce
Divorce is when a husband and wife sign legal papers that mean they are not married anymore.

Fault
If something is your fault, it means you have caused something bad to happen.

Feelings
Feelings are the way you feel about what is happening to you. You can feel happy or sad, brave or afraid, bored or excited.

Married
Two people are married when they sign papers that make them husband and wife.

Mediator
A mediator helps people who disagree to find a way to agree and make plans for the future.

Separate
Parents separate when they decide not to live together anymore and, if they are married, to get a divorce.

Single
Someone who is single isn't married. When parents get divorced, they become single again.

Splitting up
Parents split up when they decide not to live together anymore and, if they are married, to get a divorce.

Trust
When you trust someone, you know they will tell you the truth and look after you.

Worry
You worry when you don't know what is going to happen and you think of all the bad things that might happen.

FURTHER INFORMATION

Books

Harrington, Claudia. *My Two Homes*. Minneapolis, MN: Looking Glass Library, 2016.

Higgins, Melissa. *Weekends with Dad: What to Expect When Your Parents Divorce*. Mankato, MN: Picture Window Books, 2012.

Petersen, Christine. *The Smart Kid's Guide to Divorce*. Mankato, MN: The Child's World, 2015.

PowerKids Press has developed an online list of websites related to the subject of this book. This site is updated regularly. Please use this link to access the list: www.powerkidslinks.com/dw/divorce

INDEX